Gus the Greedy Puppy

Mrs Wilson burst in through the kitchen door, making everyone, including Gus, jump. She was red in the face and looked very upset indeed.

"Is something wrong, Mrs Wilson?" Holly asked.

"Yes, something's very wrong!" Mrs Wilson said angrily. "I want to complain about your dog. He's eaten my diamond ring!"

Titles in Jenny Dale's PUPPY TALES™ series

Coming Next

More of Jenny Dale's PUPPY TALES
stories follow soon

All of Jenny Dale's PUPPY TALES books can
be ordered at your local bookshop or are
available by post from Book Service by Post
(tel: 01624 675137)

Gus the Greedy Puppy

by Jenny Dale

Illustrated by Frank Rodgers

A Working Partners Book

MACMILLAN CHILDREN'S BOOKS

To Beulah, who was the bravest of puppies

First published 1999 by Macmillan Children's Books
a division of Macmillan Publishers Limited
25 Eccleston Place, London SW1W 9NF
Basingstoke and Oxford

Associated companies throughout the world

Created by Working Partners Limited
London W12 7QY

ISBN 0 330 37359 5

1 3 5 7 9 8 6 4 2

A CIP catalogue record for this book is available from
the British Library.

Typeset by Macmillan Children's Books
Printed by Mackays of Chatham plc, Kent

Chapter One

"Gus! Stop that!"

Gus didn't stop. He was enjoying himself. He'd found one of Mr Carter's ties lying on the bedroom floor and he was chewing it to bits.

"Gus!" Holly shouted again as she ran up the stairs towards him. "Give me that!"

No way! Gus thought. He hung on to one end of the tattered tie as Holly grabbed the other, and they both began to pull.

"Let go, Gus!" Holly squealed. "Dad's going to be mad when he sees what you've done!"

Gus couldn't understand why. After all, Holly's dad only put the tie round his neck. It didn't *do* anything. Gus could have much more fun with it!

"*Gus!*"

At the sound of Mrs Carter's stern voice behind him, Gus suddenly decided that he'd had enough fun with Mr Carter's tie after all. He let go, and Holly fell backwards, landing on her bottom.

"Oh no! It *would* be his favourite tie!" Mrs Carter stared sternly at the puppy. "You're a very naughty boy, Gus!"

Gus decided it was time for his best "I'm sorry" look. He slumped down and put his head on his paws. His big brown eyes looked sadly up at Mrs Carter and Holly.

"Oh, isn't he sweet?" Holly knelt down and cuddled him. Gus wagged his tail joyfully and rolled over to let her tickle his fat little tummy.

"He's a monster," Mrs Carter said, but she was trying not to smile. "Here, Holly, you'd better go and put this in the bin. And let's hope your dad doesn't notice it's gone. He still hasn't realised his leather gloves have disappeared too."

Gus wondered if they'd found Mr Carter's slippers – the ones he'd hidden behind the sofa to have a quiet chew on when he was bored. He hoped not. He'd hardly started on the left one yet.

Holly went downstairs with the

remains of the tie, and Gus raced after her. He was hungry, and he was sure it was time for his next meal. He bounced into the kitchen and sat down hopefully by his empty bowl.

"Oh, Gus!" sighed Mrs Carter as she followed them in. "You can't be hungry again." She looked at the clock. "You only had your lunch half an hour ago!"

Gus couldn't understand what the round thing on the wall had to do with whether he was fed or not. He glared up at it, wishing he could reach it – he'd chew it to bits!

"Here, Gus," Holly whispered, slipping him a dog biscuit while her mother was busy at the sink.

Gus wolfed it down gratefully
and gave her a big lick on the
nose. Holly giggled and hugged
him.

"That dog could win a gold
medal for eating!" Mrs Carter
shook her head as she turned on
the taps. "And what he doesn't
eat, he chews!"

But I'm hungry! Gus thought
grumpily. He barked a few times,
but Mrs Carter shook her head.

"No, Gus. You've had quite
enough."

"No, I haven't," Gus woofed to
himself. He waited until Mrs
Carter and Holly were busy
doing the washing-up, then he
trotted out of the kitchen door
into the back garden.

It was a warm sunny day, but
Gus didn't even stop to chase the
butterflies. He hurried over to the
fence and wriggled through a
small gap he'd found into Mr
Smith's garden.

Mr Smith was sitting in a
deckchair with a plate of cheese
sandwiches on his knee. Gus
was delighted. He loved cheese
sandwiches. He bounded over to
Mr Smith, barking a greeting.

"Hello, Gus." The old man put down his newspaper and patted the puppy on the head. "How did you know I was having my lunch? You always arrive at just the right moment!"

Gus shared Mr Smith's plate of cheese sandwiches, then he said goodbye and went next door to the Burtons' house.

Emma, who was in Holly's class at school, was playing in the garden with her little brother Paul. Jock, their Westie, was there too. Emma and Paul were eating salt and vinegar crisps. Gus's favourite flavour was cheese and onion, but he liked salt and vinegar too, so he hurried over to them.

"Oh no, not you again!" Jock

barked, as Emma and Paul made a big fuss of Gus. "Doesn't Holly feed you?"

"Of course she does!" Gus growled as he crunched up all the crisps the children were giving him. "But I'm still hungry!"

Gus stayed until all the crisps were finished, then moved on. Mr Graham, who lived at Number 7, wasn't at home, but Gus got some chicken from Mrs Patel at Number 9 and a rusk from the baby at Number 11.

By now, Gus was beginning to feel quite full. He decided it was time to go home. There was only one house left in the row anyway, and it wasn't on Gus's usual round. Mrs Wilson, who lived at

Number 13, didn't like dogs.
Instead she had a snooty white
Persian cat called Lulu, who
walked up and down the street
with her nose in the air.

Gus was about to head for
home when he smelt something.
He stopped in his tracks and
sniffed. He sniffed again. It was a
delicious smell, warm and fruity
and spicy. And it was coming
from Mrs Wilson's house.

Gus had to find out what it was.
He hurried back across the lawn
of Number 11 to look for a gap in
the fence he'd noticed, leading
into Mrs Wilson's garden.

It was rather a squeeze, but
Gus managed to push his way
through. The kitchen door stood

open, and the smell was getting stronger and more delicious by the minute.

Gus crept up to the doorway and peeped inside. He didn't want to meet Mrs Wilson or Lulu. But the kitchen was empty.

Something was bubbling away in a big pan on top of the cooker and, on the big wooden table, Gus could see a big cake and lots of little pies and tarts, cooling on a wire rack.

Licking his lips, Gus padded softly into the kitchen. He jumped up onto one of the kitchen chairs and put his paws on the table. He didn't know where to start! As well as the cake, there were custard tarts – another of Gus's favourites. And next to a big bowl of pastry mix with a wooden spoon stuck in it, Gus spotted chocolate chip cookies!

But the big sponge cake with jam in the middle was nearest. Just as Gus opened his mouth to take a big bite out of it, Mrs Wilson walked into the kitchen with Lulu in her arms.

"Eeek!" Mrs Wilson screamed when she saw Gus. "Get away from my cake, you horrid little dog!"

"How dare you come into my house!" Lulu hissed at him, showing her sharp teeth.

Frightened, Gus jumped down and ran for the door. He rushed

back through the gap in the fence
into Number 11's garden, and
through all the other gardens, not
stopping until he was safely back
home.

"Gus, I've been looking for you!"
Holly said as Gus trotted into the
kitchen. "Where've you been?"

"I can guess," said Mrs Carter.
"On his usual round of visits to
the neighbours!"

"Gus, have you been begging
for food again?" Holly asked
sternly.

Gus opened his eyes wide and
tried to look as if he'd never
dream of doing such a thing.

Holly couldn't help laughing.
"You're a bad boy!" she said,
stroking his soft coat.

"It's lucky our neighbours like him," Mrs Carter remarked, "or they'd be complaining all the time!"

Right at that moment Mrs Wilson burst in through the kitchen door, making everyone, including Gus, jump. She was red in the face and looked very upset indeed.

"Is something wrong, Mrs Wilson?" Holly asked.

"Yes, something's very wrong!" Mrs Wilson said angrily. "I want to complain about your dog. He's eaten my diamond ring!"

Chapter Two

"*What?*" gasped Holly and Mrs Carter together.

Gus looked puzzled. He didn't even know what a diamond ring was. But whatever it was, he was sure he hadn't eaten it. He hadn't eaten anything in Mrs Wilson's kitchen.

"He's eaten my diamond ring!"
Mrs Wilson said again.

"Gus wouldn't eat a *ring*," Holly
said.

"Why not?" Mrs Wilson
snapped. "That dog eats anything!
He ate all the heads off my
daffodils once!"

"And they tasted *horrible*!" Gus
barked indignantly.

"Gus, be quiet!" said Mrs Carter.
Then she turned to Mrs Wilson.
"Why do you think Gus is to
blame, Mrs Wilson?" she asked.

"Because I found him climbing
onto my kitchen table about five
minutes ago!" Mrs Wilson said
crossly. "I'd taken my ring off and
left it on the table while I was

baking. When I came back, it was
gone!"

Mrs Wilson suddenly looked
very sad. "The ring was a present
from my husband," she said
quietly. "It's very precious to me.
I simply *must* get it back."

"I'm sorry, Mrs Wilson," Holly
said. "But I'm sure Gus didn't eat
your ring."

Gus licked Holly's hand gratefully.

Mrs Wilson shook her head. "He *must* have done!" she declared.

"It *wasn't* me!" Gus howled. "Your stuck-up cat could have eaten the ring!"

"Be *quiet*, Gus!" Mrs Carter said sharply.

Gus shut up. He hadn't seen Holly's mum get quite so angry before, and it scared him.

"I suppose Gus *might* have eaten the ring," Mrs Carter said slowly. "He does like to eat very odd things sometimes."

"Oh, *Mum*!" Holly said. "Gus wouldn't eat a diamond ring. Not if there were cakes and biscuits lying about."

"He would have hoovered up everything on the table if I hadn't walked in just then!" Mrs Wilson said furiously. "That dog's a menace!"

Gus couldn't be quiet any longer, and he barked loudly. It wasn't fair! He hadn't eaten Mrs Wilson's nasty old ring, and he didn't see why he should get the blame.

"Gus, be *quiet*!" shouted Mrs Carter. "Holly, go and shut him in the living room while I talk to Mrs Wilson."

"That dog needs to be taught some manners!" Mrs Wilson sniffed.

"Sit down, Mrs Wilson, and I'll make you a nice cup of tea," Holly's mum said. "Then we can talk about how we can find your ring."

Holly took Gus's collar and pulled him out of the kitchen. Gus dug his claws in because he didn't want to leave. He wanted to stay there and tell Mrs Wilson exactly what he thought of her. But in the end he gave in, and let Holly take him into the living room.

"Oh, Gus," Holly sighed, kneeling down to put her arms around him. "I wish you hadn't gone into Mrs Wilson's kitchen."

"So do I," Gus woofed miserably as he snuggled into her arms. "Then I wouldn't be in this mess!"

"If only you could talk!" Holly went on, looking just as miserable. "Then you could tell

us what really happened."

Gus whined, and put his paw on Holly's arm. He hated to see her so sad. And it was all his fault. That made him feel even worse.

"I'll go and see what Mum and Mrs Wilson are saying," Holly told him. "Be a good boy, Gus, and don't make a noise."

She went out, closing the door behind her. Gus slumped down on the carpet and put his nose between his paws. He felt very sad indeed. If only he hadn't been so greedy, none of this would have happened. Now he had made Holly unhappy – and he'd made Mrs Carter very angry.

Suddenly Gus sat up, feeling frightened. What if Mrs Carter was *so* angry with him that he was sent back to the Dogs' Home? Gus had been born at the home and had lived there until, one day, the Carters had come looking for a puppy and had chosen him. That had been the happiest day of Gus's life.

The Dogs' Home was big and noisy and crowded. The people there were very busy. They didn't have time to play with him like Holly did. Gus didn't want to go back there. Besides, he loved Holly more than anyone else in the whole world, and he didn't want to leave her. So there was only one thing to do . . .

Gus jumped up. He must find Mrs Wilson's diamond ring himself, and show everyone that he hadn't eaten it!

Chapter Three

Gus looked round the living
room, wondering how he could
get out. The door was closed, but
one of the windows was open just
a little. Gus knew he wasn't
allowed on the furniture, but this
was an emergency. He leapt onto
the big armchair near the window

and scrambled up its back and onto the windowsill.

Gus nudged the window open a little wider with his nose and looked out. It seemed an awfully long way down and he felt rather nervous about jumping. But then Gus remembered Holly's sad face. He took a deep breath, jumped . . .

. . . and landed safely in the soft earth of the flowerbed beneath the window.

"Yes!" he barked proudly. "I did it!"

Gus picked himself up and trotted down the garden path. There was no time to waste. He had to get to Mrs Wilson's house and find the ring before something awful happened to him.

"Hey, Gus!" Jock was in the Burtons' back garden, chewing on a large juicy bone. He looked up as Gus raced past. "Do you want a lick? There's plenty here for two!"

Gus shook his head. "I'm not hungry!" he called, and didn't stop. He didn't care if he never saw a bone again, as long as he didn't have to leave Holly and go back to the Dogs' Home.

Jock was so surprised he dropped the bone. It rolled into the Burtons' fish pond, and Jock didn't even notice. "Gus isn't hungry?" he barked. "I don't believe it!"

When Gus reached the gap in the fence leading to Mrs Wilson's garden he skidded to a halt, panting hard. Then he squeezed through the gap and trotted up the path to the kitchen door, looking carefully around him in case Mrs Wilson was already on her way back home.

But this time the kitchen door was closed. Gus's heart sank. He should have guessed that Mrs Wilson would lock up her house before she left. But he had to find a way in. He had to.

Keeping a nervous lookout for Lulu, Gus went to investigate the back of the house. Gus wasn't the only dog in the street who was scared of Lulu. He'd seen the hefty white cat take on dogs before. She sent them running home with their tails between their legs as soon as she lashed out with her razor-sharp claws. But luckily Lulu was nowhere to be seen.

All the windows at the back of the house were closed. Gus ran up and down trying to find a way in, but there was not even a tiny gap he could squeeze through.

Gloomily Gus went back to the kitchen door again. What was he going to do? Somehow he had to get into that house, or he might be back in the Dogs' Home before he could say "Woof". And then he'd never see Holly again . . .

Gus whined and stood up on his back legs, putting his front paws on the kitchen door. He pushed at it as hard as he could, but it didn't move. It was then that Gus noticed something at the bottom of the door. Lulu's cat flap!

Gus was so excited that he had to stop himself from barking out loud. Eagerly he pushed his nose against the flap. It moved, and Gus stuck his head through into Mrs Wilson's kitchen. Now for the rest of him . . .

Carefully Gus began to make his way through the hole in the door. He wriggled and he pushed and he just about got his front paws and shoulders inside. It was a very tight fit.

Gus tried to get his other half through the cat flap. He wriggled and he pulled, but he couldn't move. He tried again and again, but his tummy was too big to get through the hole. He was stuck!

Gus began to feel very frightened. He didn't know what to do. He couldn't get in and he couldn't get out.

Then behind him he heard a silky voice say, "And what do you think you're doing in *my* cat flap?"

Chapter Four

It was Lulu! Gus began to
tremble with fear.

"You look very silly indeed,"
Lulu said. Gus could almost
hear her sharpening her claws
gleefully. "I think you'd better
come out, right now."

"I can't!" Gus whined miserably.

"I'm stuck!"

"Serves you right for eating the diamond ring!" Lulu sniffed.

"I *didn't* eat it!" Gus said indignantly. "I've come to look for it. And – and I've got to find it because if I don't, I might get sent back to the Dogs' Home and then I'll never see Holly again . . ."

Lulu didn't say anything, and Gus began to feel even more nervous. He couldn't see what the cat was doing behind him, but he didn't want to stay and find out. He began to wriggle about again, trying to get through the cat flap into Mrs Wilson's kitchen.

"Keep still!" Lulu hissed at him. "You'll never get in that way –

you're too fat! You'd better try
and come out again."

Gus knew that Lulu was right.
He was just too big to get through
the cat flap. "But I can't get out
again either!" he wailed.

"Yes, you can!" Lulu said
crossly. "You got in, didn't you?
Just take it slowly."

Gus began trying to ease himself
gently backwards. At first he
didn't move at all. He pulled
harder . . . and harder . . . Then, all
of a sudden, he shot backwards
out of the cat flap like a cork out of
a bottle, and tumbled head over
heels onto the path.

"Thank you!" he woofed.

Lulu, who was having a wash,
gave him a bored look. "Dogs!"

she yawned. "They're so stupid! I can show you a much better way to get into the house."

Gus stared at the cat in amazement.

"You want to get into the house, don't you?" Lulu jumped onto a dustbin which stood underneath the kitchen windows. She began pulling at the smallest window with her claws and, after a minute or two, it swung open.

"The catch is broken," explained Lulu as she leapt down onto the path again. "If you can get up there, you can climb into the kitchen quite easily."

Gus could hardly believe his ears. Lulu, the cat who hated dogs, was helping him?

"Thank you!" he said. "But – but why are you helping me like this?"

"I came from the Cats' Home," Lulu said quietly. "I wouldn't want to go back there either!"

The dustbin was quite tall, but there was a big black bag of rubbish lying next to it. Gus climbed onto the bag first and then managed to get onto the dustbin. From there, it was easy for him to jump up onto the windowsill.

He peered through the window into Mrs Wilson's kitchen. Just below him was the sink and draining board, which was piled with clean plates and cups.

Gus hopped down carefully onto the edge of the sink, but felt his front paw skidding on the slippery surface. *CRASH!*

As Gus knocked against the pile of crockery, plates and cups flew everywhere and smashed to bits as they hit the floor.

"I think that's called a crash landing," Lulu remarked as she came in through the cat flap.

"Oh, no!" Gus muttered. "How did *that* happen?" He inspected his paw. He'd trodden on a drop of spilt washing-up liquid. No wonder he'd slipped!

He jumped down off the draining board. It wasn't a very good start. Still, he was sure Mrs Wilson would forgive him if he found her diamond ring.

"Where are you going to start looking?" Lulu asked.

"I . . . er . . . don't quite know."

Gus suddenly realised that he didn't even know what a diamond ring was.

Lulu sighed. "You do *know* what a diamond ring is, don't you?"

"No," said Gus sadly.

Lulu told him. Gus couldn't help feeling alarmed when he found out how small it was. He looked around the enormous kitchen. How would he find a tiny little thing like a diamond ring in here? But he had to try, for Holly's sake.

First Gus went over to the kitchen table. He remembered that Mrs Wilson said she'd left her ring there when she'd started cooking. All the cakes and biscuits and the big bowl of pastry mix were still there, but Gus wasn't interested in food. He jumped up onto a chair and nosed around, looking for the ring.

CRASH! Lulu jumped as Gus accidentally knocked the plate of chocolate chip cookies onto the floor.

"Be careful!" she hissed.

Gus didn't care. He had to find that ring. But there was no sign of it on the kitchen table.

Next Gus sniffed his way all round the kitchen floor, in case the ring had fallen off the table. It hadn't.

Then he looked in all the cupboards he could reach. It wasn't easy, because it took him a long time to get each one open.

The cupboards were so full of tins, bottles and packets of food that things kept falling out onto the floor.

Meanwhile, Lulu looked in all the places Gus couldn't reach, like the top of the fridge and the high shelves on the wall. But they didn't find the ring.

"It's not here!" Gus slumped down miserably on the kitchen floor. "What am I going to do?"

"We'd better get out of here," Lulu said, looking around the kitchen, "or we're going to be in big trouble."

Gus looked around the kitchen too, and his heart sank. It was a mess. The floor was covered with bits of broken crockery and cookies, along with tins and packets of food. What on earth would Mrs Wilson say when she saw it?

Lulu was right. They had to get out of there, and fast – before Mrs Wilson came back.

Then, suddenly, Gus's ears pricked up. He could hear Holly's voice! He listened harder. Now he could hear Mrs Carter and Mrs Wilson talking as well. The voices were coming closer and closer. Gus could hear footsteps too.

Mrs Wilson and Holly and her mum were walking up the path to Mrs Wilson's kitchen door!

Gus panicked. He ran over to the sink, but the draining board was too high for him to jump onto.

"Hide!" Lulu hissed, her tail swinging wildly from side to side.

Gus looked frantically around for somewhere to hide, but it was too late. The voices were already outside the back door!

Chapter Five

"But I've looked *everywhere*," Mrs Wilson was saying, as she put her key into the lock. "I tell you, that puppy of yours *must* have eaten it!"

"Gus can be a bit naughty at times, Mrs Wilson," Holly admitted, "but I'm *sure* he wouldn't have eaten your ring."

"Let's have another look for it," Mrs Carter added. "Holly and I will help you."

"It won't do any good," Mrs Wilson sniffed, sounding rather tearful as she pushed open the kitchen door. "I know exactly where my ring is – inside your dog's tummy! I'm never going to get it back . . ." The door swung open.

"Oh, no!" Mrs Wilson stopped dead in the doorway. "Look at my kitchen!" she wailed.

"Well, everyone makes a bit of a mess when they're baking," said Mrs Carter, trying not to look shocked.

"I didn't do this!" Mrs Wilson

cried. "Ooh! And look at all my crockery!" she shouted, as she noticed the mess by the sink.

Then suddenly she spotted Gus, who was trying to hide under the kitchen table. "Aha! I might have known!" Her face red with fury, Mrs Wilson bent down under the table, grabbed Gus's collar and pulled him out.

"Gus!" Holly gasped. "How on earth did you get in here?"

Gus whined. He was in real trouble now.

"Never mind how he got in here!" Mrs Wilson retorted, still keeping a tight hold of Gus's collar. "Somehow he did, and just *look* at the mess he's made. *And* he's scared my cat!"

Lulu, who was sitting on top of the fridge watching what was going on, miaowed loudly. "He didn't scare *me*!" she said, offended that anyone could think she found a mere puppy scary.

"I'm so sorry, Mrs Wilson," said Holly's mum quickly. "I just don't understand how Gus got in. We'll pay for the damage, of course."

"Maybe he came to look for the ring," Holly said.

"Oh, very funny!" snorted Mrs Wilson rudely.

"Don't be silly, Holly," said her mum.

"I'm not!" Holly insisted. "Maybe Gus was just trying to help."

Gus gave a yelp. At least Holly believed in him. He tried to pull away from Mrs Wilson, so that he could rush over to Holly and give her another grateful lick, but Mrs Wilson was holding his collar too tightly. In fact, she was holding it so tightly, it was beginning to hurt. Gus pulled harder, trying to get away.

"Now I want to know what

you're going to do about this . . . this animal!" Mrs Wilson demanded. "He's eaten my precious ring and messed up my kitchen, and I've just about had enough!"

Gus made one last effort to get away from Mrs Wilson. Dragging her with him, Gus lunged forward towards Holly.

"Aah!" Mrs Wilson screamed again as she fell against the table. The bowl of pastry mix toppled off and hit the floor with a great clatter. Big splodges of sticky yellow pastry mix flew everywhere, especially over Gus and Mrs Wilson.

"Look what he's done!" Mrs Wilson spluttered furiously as she tried to wipe the pastry crumbs off her face. "That dog should be locked up – he's dangerous!"

"Oh, Gus!" Holly sighed. "What have you done *now*?"

But Gus wasn't listening. He could see something glittering in the pastry mix on the floor.

Chapter Six

"I want that dog out of my kitchen *now*!" Mrs Wilson shouted angrily.

"Come on, Gus." Holly hurried across the kitchen towards him. "I think we'd better go."

Gus took no notice. He pushed his nose into the heap of pastry mix and barked loudly.

Holly knelt down beside him. "What are you doing, Gus?" she asked.

Gus barked again and scrabbled in the pastry mix with his paws.

Then Holly suddenly saw what he was trying to show her. "It's the ring!" she shouted, picking it up. "Gus has found the ring!"

"*What*?" Mrs Wilson's eyes almost popped out of her head. "Let me see that!"

She grabbed the sticky, pastry-covered ring, rushed over to the tap and rinsed it clean. "It *is* my ring! Oh, thank goodness," she said in a shaky voice. "I thought it had gone for ever!"

"It must have fallen into the

bowl of pastry mix!" said Mrs
Carter.

"It's a good job you didn't make
that pastry into pies, Mrs Wilson,"
said Holly. "The ring would have
been inside, and someone might
have *really* eaten it!"

Mrs Wilson turned pale at the
very thought and had to sit down
on one of the kitchen chairs.

"Well done, Gus!" Holly said
proudly, giving her puppy a big
hug. "We'd never have found the
ring if it wasn't for you!"

Gus began to bark joyfully.
Thank goodness he'd managed to
get himself out of trouble. But it
had been a close thing!

Mrs Wilson looked round at the
mess in her kitchen and frowned.

"It was really very naughty of you to come into my kitchen, Gus," she said.

Gus hung his head. If he hadn't been so greedy in the first place, none of this would have happened.

Then Mrs Wilson smiled. "But it was very clever of you to find my ring!" She slipped the ring onto her finger, then bent down and patted Gus on the head.

Gus licked her hand. Maybe now he and Mrs Wilson could be friends.

"We'll help you clean up the kitchen, Mrs Wilson," said Holly.

Mrs Wilson looked pleased. "Thank you, Holly," she said.

Holly and her mum helped to tidy up. Then, carrying the big wedges of jam sponge Mrs Wilson had cut and wrapped for them, along with a pile of chocolate chip cookies, they said goodbye.

"From now on, there will always be a little something for you here, when you're feeling peckish, Gus," Mrs Wilson said. "It's the least I can do!"

"Yippee!" Gus barked happily.

"Just don't get any ideas about scoffing my cat food," Lulu purred quietly from the top of the fridge.

When they got back home, Mrs Carter went straight over to the fridge and took out a big, juicy bone. "I think Gus deserves a reward for finding Mrs Wilson's ring!" she said with a smile.

"So do I!" said Holly. She took the bone and held it out to Gus. "Here you are, Gus! Good boy!"

Holly and her mum couldn't believe their eyes when Gus ignored the bone. Instead he flung himself at Holly, licking her hand and wagging his tail.

"Oh, Gus!" Holly laughed,

dropping the bone and scooping her puppy into her arms. "Aren't you hungry?"

"Of course he's hungry!" Mrs Carter laughed. "Gus is always hungry!"

But for once, Gus didn't care about the big, juicy bone. He was just glad to be back home safely, with Holly.

If he hadn't found Mrs Wilson's ring, he might have been on his way back to the Dogs' Home right now . . .

. . . *And if I hadn't been so greedy in the first place, I wouldn't have got into so much trouble,* Gus thought. *I'm not going to be so greedy ANY MORE!*

"I really don't think Gus wants

this bone, Mum," said Holly.

Mrs Carter looked surprised.
"Oh well, put it back in the fridge,
and he can have it later," she said.
"Maybe Gus has decided to
change his ways!"

"I have!" Gus yapped happily as
Holly gave him a cuddle. "I still
love food, but not as much as I
love you, Holly!"

He gave her a lick, then looked
at her hopefully. "But when my
appetite comes back," he woofed,
"I'd be more than happy to help
out with that jam sponge!"

Collect all of JENNY DALE'S PUPPY TALES!

The prices shown below are correct at the time of going to press. However, Macmillan Publishers reserve the right to show new retail prices on covers which may differ from those previously advertised.

JENNY DALE'S PUPPY TALES

MORE PUPPY TALES BOOKS FOLLOW SOON!

All Macmillan titles can be ordered at your local bookshop or are available by post from:

Book Service by Post
PO Box 29, Douglas, Isle of Man IM99 1BQ

Credit cards accepted. For details:
Telephone: 01624 675137
Fax: 01624 670923
E-mail: bookshop@enterprise.net

Free postage and packing in the UK.
Overseas customers: add £1 per book (paperback)
and £3 per book (hardback).